D0457705

Focus on the Family PRESENTS

McGEE and me! ™

Take Me Out of the Ball Game

Bill Myers

1 on characters created by Bill Myers and Ken C. Johnson; story by Ken C. Johnson, Rob Loos, and George Taweel; and the teleplay by April Dammann

Tyndale House Publishers, Inc.
Wheaton, Illinois

For Dan Johnson

Front cover illustration copyright © 1990 by Morgan Weistling
Interior illustrations by Nathan Greene, copyright © 1990
by Tyndale House Publishers, Inc.

Library of Congress Catalog Card Number 90-70611
ISBN 0-8423-4113-7
McGee and Me!, McGee, and McGee and Me! logo
are trademarks of Living Bibles International
Copyright © 1990 by Living Bibles International
All rights reserved
Printed in the United States of America

02   01   00   99   98   97
12   11   10   9   8   7

Contents

LIBRARY
DEXTER SCHOOLS
DEXTER, NM 88230

Don't look to men for help; their greatest leaders fail. . . . But happy is the man who has the God of Jacob as his helper, whose hope is in the Lord his God. (Psalm 146: 3, 5, *The Living Bible*)

ONE
Time Tracker to the Rescue

Although worn and weary, my wonderfully worthy body stumbled into the nearest 7-Eleven. What a day! All I needed now was to drown my sorrows in a couple dozen cans of Diet Pepsi, three bags of Chee-tos, eight packages of Twinkies, and a dozen or so Gooey Chewy bars. That should hold me over during the twenty-minute drive home to dinner.

But, back to my day. As the most experienced (and, of course, the best dressed) Time Tracker this side of the twenty-third century, I had been chosen to time-port back to the 1800s. It seems some writer-type guy by the name of Hands Christian Anderson was having problems with one of his kids' stories. It was about this little girl fish falling in love with a sailor.

"Dis is one lu-lu of an ideea," he kept saying. "And I sink I'll call et 'De Liddle Sardine.'"

"No, Handsy-boy, Sweetheart, Babe," I argued in my best Hollywoodeese. "You got to think splashier, more sensational. You got to think big, big, BIG!"

"Big?" he asked. Then after a moment his eyes lit up. "Yumppen Yimminie, I got et! I can see et now. I'll call et 'De Liddle Whale!'"

I let out a sigh and murmured, "Mermaid . . . What about 'The Little Mermaid'?"

He shook his head fiercely. "Nah . . . dat vill never sell."

We argued all day and night. Back and forth. Forth and back. Talk about stubborn . . . if this guy was any more bullheaded he'd be sprouting horns and chasing red capes.

Finally he gave in. But only after I promised to bring a Big Mac and a side of fries the next time I dropped by his century.

Yes-siree-bob, another dramatic job dynamically done. As usual, I was mesmerized by my incredible ingenuity while I reached over to press the portable Time Transporter strapped to my wrist. But just as my finger reached the button, my keen eye spotted another book.

"What's this, Handsy?" I asked.

"Dat's my next masterpiece," he beamed. "Et's all about dis princess and all dees mattresses she has to sleep on and—"

"What's it called?" I interrupted, somehow fearing the worst.

"I call et," he gave a big proud grin, "I call et 'De Princess and de Watermelon'!"

I released the button on my wrist and let out a sigh. It was going to be another long day.

But all of that was behind me now. Now I was in my favorite 7-Eleven about to eat my weight in chips, candies, and cakes. It was a junk-food junkie's dream.

But wait a minute, something was wrong! That smell. Instead of the wondrous aroma of deep-fried and cholesterol-coated goodies, I smelled, oh no! Could it be . . . but, yes, yes . . . horror of horrors . . . it was . . .

HEALTH FOOD!

I spun around and let out a gasp. Behind me were rows and rows of fresh fruits and vegetables. Everywhere I looked there was food that was actually healthy to eat. Suddenly my dream was turning into a nightmare.

I could feel my body begin to tremble. Such healthy munchies were more than I could manage. "Where . . . where's the junk food?" I nervously stuttered to the clerk.

"Junk food?" he asked blankly.

"Yeah, you know, like candy, chips, and all those other wonderful artery pluggers?"

"Well, the celery chips are in aisle three and the carrot candy is over in aisle—"

"NO, NO, NO!" I shouted. My whole body was beginning to shake. I was going through junk food withdrawal. If I didn't consume a good hit of empty calories in the next few minutes, it was going to get ugly. My wonderful layers of fat would start to dissolve, my chances of a stroke (or at least a good bypass operation) would disappear forever. "Please," I begged. "I need something sweet and crunchy!!"

"Well, we have some raisins and granola bars over in—"

"NO! YOU NINNY!!" I shouted, grabbing his collar

and pulling him directly into my face. "I'm talking GREASE!! Sensational, salt-saturated, sugar-sprinkled, deep-fried GREASE!!!"

But the look on his face said he'd never heard the word. Somehow the phrase "junk food" had not made it into his vocabulary. And then it hit me . . .

Dr. Dastardly!!!!

Of course. My arch rival, the twisted Time Traveler who treks back in time to foul up history. The boisterous bad guy who was responsible for you having to go to school five days a week with two days off. (It's true. The guy who originally invented school wanted it the other way around, two days of school and five days off.) The vile villain responsible for creating that secret ingredient in milk shakes that gives you headaches when you drink them too fast. And, worst of all worsts, the fiendish fiend responsible for those ridiculous prices they charge at theaters for soda pop and candy.

He had struck again. But this was by far his worst blow to humanity. Dr. Dastardly had gone back in time and somehow uninvented junk food!

Quicker than you can say "polyunsaturated," I reached into my coat and pulled out my time chart. Ah-ha, just as I figured. Dastardly's homing device showed him back in 1914. I locked onto his quadrants, pressed my Transporter button and—

Snap-Crackle-Zit!

I was in 1914.

Sure enough, there in front of me was Doc Dastardly. And he was standing beside the world-renowned food inventor—the founding father of junk food—the one and only Professor Potat O.

Chip. True to form, the honorable gourmet was hovering over his vat of boiling oil. But he was not trying to make potato chips. Somehow Dastardly had convinced him to give up on potatoes and start working with cauliflower!

"Dastardly," I called, my voice shaky and my stomach already churning over the thought of cauliflower chips.

He spun around and looked at me. "I knew you'd come," he sneered, and I could tell he'd gotten an A in the Sleazy Sneer class at Bad Guy School. "It's been a long time."

"Ever since Book #4," I agreed. But this wasn't a time for nostalgia. I had a job to do and, as usual, I'd do it well. "So are you going to come quietly," I asked, "or do I have to—" But I never finished the sentence.

Suddenly he raised a fresh raw carrot to his lips. Before I could scream in protest he chomped down and took a bite out of the hopelessly healthful vegetable.

The pain was fierce, but I carried on. With an uproarious roar I raced toward the vile, villainous villain. But he threw everything he had at me—first he ate pitted prunes . . . then fresh turnip greens. . . . Next came the asparagus and raw broccoli.

I began to stagger. The pain was too much. Everything began to spin. I was about to pass out.

Seeing I was on the ropes, he quickly downed three cans of V-8 juice in the hopes of finishing me off. He nearly succeeded. And yet, somehow, remarkably (and, of course, quite heroically) I continued to stagger forward.

Finally he reached into his Spandex muscle shirt and pulled out his secret weapon. It was a bag of vitamins! I gasped in horror. "No!" I begged. "Not that. Please, please anything but—"

He let out another sinister laugh and then started pelting them at me. A B-12 there, a Vitamin C here, and then there was the dreaded iron supplement. The pain was just too much. I fell to my knees in agony as the horrendous pills of pure health pelted my pudgy body. And yet miraculously I managed to hang on. (I had to, I have eight more chapters to go in this book.)

Then I saw it. A remnant from the good old days. A reminder of when I and the rest of the world could stuff ourselves to oblivious obesity. It was a crumb—from a corn chip. It was stuck to my argyle sock. I reached for it with trembling hands of thankfulness.

Now it was the Doc's turn to gasp in horror.

Quicker than you can say Frito-Lay, I rose to my feet. A grin of victory spread across my perfect pearlies as I began to approach the quivering mass of cowardice.

"No," he screamed. "Get away—get away with that!"

I continued to head for him, holding the corn chip crumb before me. Of course, I desperately wanted to eat the delightful delicacy. But I was made of firmer (or is it flabbier?) stuff than that.

Then it happened. I was less than four feet away when I stepped on a pile of rutabagas. My nimble feet flew out from under me and sent me crashing to the floor.

Dastardly jumped up and leaped on me. Now we were in each other's grip, locked in mortal, hand-to-hand combat. But as fiercely as my foe fought, it was his breath that nearly killed me. (The man had obviously slipped some parsley into his mouth when I wasn't looking, and now everything smelled fresh and wholesome.)

Then, just when I was about to do what every super-hero and all-around good-looking good guy does—destroy evil (or at least mess up its hair a lot)—the dastardly Doc hit his Time Transporter and—Snap-Crackle-Zit!—he disappeared into another century.

Rats! I hate it when he does that.

Who knew what sinister schemes his slimy soul was scheming—what terrifying trauma he would be touting? But that was OK. Once again good had triumphed over evil. Once again your handsomely heroic hero beat your villainous villain. And once again the world would be a sweeter, crunchier, and slightly saltier place to live in.

"Yo, Professor," I said, tossing a spud across the room into Mr. Potato Head's vat of boiling oil. "Have a few empty carbos on me. I'd love to stick around, but I have a little shopping to do. . . . " With that I reached to my Time Transporter and—

Snap-Crackle-Zit!

Pig-out city, here I come. . . .

TWO

"Take Me Out to the Ball Game . . ."

Things were not going well for little Roger Goreman. Not well at all. For years the little guy had dreamed of being a film director. That's all he wanted. Just to take his folks' video camera and make movies. Shucks, if it made his dad happy he wouldn't even mind making movies of sporting events.

What he did mind was being made to *play* in those events. What he minded even more was that he was standing at home plate with two strikes against him. And what he minded most of all was that it was the last inning of the game, his team was one run behind, and everyone was depending upon him to knock the tying run home and score so they could win the Eastfield City Championship.

Nope. It was not a good day for little Roger Goreman.

Come to think of it, it wasn't such a hot day for Mr. Martin, Nicholas's dad, either. This was Mr.

16

Martin's second year coaching. For two years now he had been working with the kids—teaching them to field, to hit, to run bases. And now it all came down to little Roger Goreman, the weakest link in the Eastfield Braves Little League team.

"C'mon, Roger babe, you can do it. Concentrate now . . . concentrate. Bear down, man, he's all yours, babe, a piece of cake, you can do it."

At least that's what Dad was saying on the outside. On the inside he was saying: "We're sunk, we're dead, we're history."

Roger stepped closer to the plate. He took a few practice swings and waited. He tried to swallow, but there was nothing left to swallow. Apparently all the moisture in his body had migrated to the palms of his hands.

The grandstands were roaring with anxious moms and dads.

The dugouts were filled with screaming kids.

Everyone figured it was all up to Roger. Well, almost everyone . . .

It seems Nicholas and Louis didn't even bother to get to their feet. Oh sure, they wanted to win like everyone else on the team. But they knew there was another card left to play. They knew there was a secret weapon everyone had temporarily forgotten about.

The pitcher took his windup. He checked the runner on second. And then after a pause, he let the ball fly. At first it looked like a hot sizzler right across the plate. At first it looked like the Eastfield Braves were on their way to losing another championship.

But then, miracle of miracles, the ball began to rise. Then it began to curve to the outside. Could it be? Yes! Wonder of wonders, it looked like it was going to be ball four! It looked like Roger was going to be able to walk. It looked like things were finally going right after all.

The only problem was that nobody bothered to tell Roger what it looked like. Knowing it all depended upon him, Roger didn't think about checking whether it was a strike or a ball. Instead he reared back and took a healthy swing for all he was worth.

"OH NO!" the crowd gasped.

"Strike three!" the umpire bellowed.

"It figures," Dad muttered.

But Nicholas and Louis weren't worried. That was only two outs. There was one man to go. And nobody, I mean *nobody,* could stop this man. . . .

"Bottom of the ninth, two away," the announcer's voice boomed across the speakers.

Nicholas leaned against the wall of the dugout and clasped his hands behind his head. "It's in the bag," he said to Louis with a grin.

"A walk in the park," Louis agreed, tipping his hat over his eyes.

"Next batter up for the Braves," the announcer called, "Pitcher, Thurman Miller!"

Suddenly the crowd was back on its feet shouting and clapping for joy. They had remembered what Nicholas and Louis had known all along. Now everyone was hooting and cheering in gleeful anticipation.

Well, almost everyone. . .

It seems the pitcher of the opposite team wasn't doing a lot of cheering. Neither was his coach. Come to think of it, the other eight players in the field weren't doing many handsprings, either.

All eyes turned to the Braves' dugout as Thurman Miller emerged . . . and emerged . . . and emerged some more. To call this kid "big" was like calling King Kong a slightly overfed chimp. For a thirteen-year-old, this guy was gigantic. We're not just talking tall, either. I mean, everywhere you looked on this 5′ 10″ giant there was strength and power. In fact, when he flexed, even his muscles had muscles.

He grabbed a bat and strode toward the plate. The ground shook, the umpire moved back just a step, and mothers pulled their babies in a little closer for protection.

"OK, big fella, you can do it, you can do it!" Dad was shouting. "Out of the park, big guy, out of the park!"

The pitcher for the opposing team took off his cap and wiped the beads of perspiration that had suddenly appeared on his brow. He threw a glance to the scoreboard: 4 to 3. They were ahead by one run. He looked at the runner on second. If Thurman hit a double this man would be the tying run. He looked back to Thurman. Of course, if Goliath there hit a homer, the big guy would score the winning run.

The pitcher took a deep breath and tried to swallow. But it was his turn for a dry mouth. It was his turn for sweaty palms.

Everyone waited.

Finally he started his windup. Then he fired the fastest fastball he had ever thrown in his life. It was beautiful—a sight to behold as it streaked toward the plate. *All right! Perfect pitch!* his mind was thinking.

The only problem was that that was also what Thurman was thinking. The big fellow leaned back and turned the perfect pitch into a perfect hit.

CRACK!

The ball sailed.

The jaws dropped.

And Thurman yawned. "What a bother," he muttered as he dropped the bat and started to run. "I

go to all the trouble of hitting that ball, and now I have to run around these stupid bases."

But Thurman didn't have to run. He could take his time. I don't want to say that the ball sailed too far out of the park, or that it went too high. The fact that NASA reported one of its satellites was destroyed by a round, white UFO at that exact time was probably just a coincidence.

The crowd was on its feet cheering, and Nick and Louis were high-fiving. "All right! We did it!" they shouted as Thurman rounded third and came in to home.

Everyone piled out of the dugout and raced

toward the big guy. It took a little doing—and every available player on the team—but eventually they were able to hoist Thurman up on their shoulders.

"All right, Thurman!" Nick groaned as he staggered under the weight of the big kid. "Whatta hit! Whatta play!"

"What a load!" Louis gasped as he fought to hold him up.

By now everybody was on the field shouting and slapping one another on the back. "All right! Eastfield champs! We did it! . . . Nice work!"

"Great job, Thurman," Dad called as he pushed his way through the crowd to the boy. "Everybody, you were terrific!"

The kids let out another cheer.

"Listen up . . . ," he shouted. "We're the Eastfield City Champions now!"

More shouting and cheering.

"Regional finals, here we come!" Louis yelled.

Nicholas joined in, "Then Thurman takes us right to the Little League Series!"

More cheering. Also a few groans. By the look of pain across some of the guys' faces, it definitely was time to lower Thurman back to the ground.

"Great game, son."

Louis turned around to see his mom and dad. They were a handsome couple. Like many couples their age, they were so busy with their careers that they hardly had time to be a family. Why, with Louis's mom's work as a legal secretary and his dad's job as a doctor at the clinic, they hardly had time to eat meals together, much less enjoy a

Saturday ball game. But today was different. And for that Louis was very grateful.

"You made some great plays," his dad said beaming as he reached out to shake Louis's hand.

But this was no time for just a handshake. Before his dad knew it, Louis dove in for a big-time bear hug. "Thanks!" he shouted into his father's chest.

Catching Mr. Martin's eye, Louis's dad raised his camera. "Think we ought to give some of these pictures to the *Eastfield Daily News*?"

Nick's dad grinned. After all, that was the paper he worked for. But before he could answer, Louis piped up: "Nah, give *Sports Illustrated* first crack."

The men chuckled as the boys moved off. Yes sir, victory was sweet. For both kids and grown-ups.

Oh yeah, victory's sweet all right. But what about us little guys? You know, us incurably cute imaginary cartoon character types that fellas like Nicholas draw for a little spice in their life. What about us?

Oh, I'm all for baseball, don't get me wrong. In fact, in my younger days I used to pitch for the Chicago Clubs out in Wiggley Field. That is, until I threw my arm out. You know, we looked everywhere for it, but to this day we still haven't found that arm. Luckily I was able to talk Nick into drawing me another one.

Yes-siree-bob, I'm all for baseball. But I'm also all for not being forgotten. So as ol' Nicky-boy was gathering his gear, I figured it would be a good time to mesmerize his mind with some catchy catching.

"Hey, Nick!" I shouted. "Let's see the ol' knuckle-ball!"

My little buddy stopped and nervously glanced around, hoping nobody saw me. But he didn't have much to worry about. As a figment of his imagination, there wasn't much chance that I would be seen by others.

"What are you doing here?" he demanded.

"Hey, look, bright eyes," I countered. "You're the one who brought the sketch pad."

Nick threw a glance to his backpack. Sure enough, there on top, in all of its yellow-covered and spiral-ringed glory was my home sweet home.

"C'mon!" I shouted, pounding my fist into my glove, "give me your best stuff!"

Nick hesitated a minute. Obviously the poor boy didn't want to be shown up.

"C'mon," I insisted. "Let's see the ol' slider, the ol' fastball, the ol' curveball, the ol' . . . "

And then, rising to my challenge, he let go the mightiest pitch of all times.

But I tell you, no matter how powerful the pitch, no matter how blazing the ball, no matter how many times it bounces and almost rolls to a stop before it gets to you . . . a seven-inch cartoon character trying to catch a three-inch hardball does not make for a pretty sight.

I'll save you all the gory details about how far it bashed me into the ground. Let's just say I became the first person in history who had to reach up to touch his toes. . . .

THREE

"Buy Me Some Peanuts and Cracker Jack . . . "

A few minutes later most of the Braves team was piled in front of the counter of Ingrid's Incredible Ice Cream Shop.

No one's sure how going to the shop ended up being a tradition. Originally, Dad used to take the team out for pizza every time they won. But that was last year. Back in the good ol' days when, if they were lucky, the team might win one or two games. Then they got better. A lot better. And, as the team got better, Dad got cheaper.

"Great," Louis had muttered, "next year he'll probably just buy us gum balls."

At least for now it was ice cream. And everyone was chowing down. Especially Thurman.

"Don't you have any bigger dishes?" he asked as he sprinkled what must have been the 100th topping on his quadruple-decker.

"We've got a bucket in the back," Ingrid said with a grin.

Thurman didn't hear. He was concentrating on finding room for topping number 101.

Meanwhile, off in the corner, Nicholas and Louis were doing what they did best. They were bugging each other. It wasn't the type of bugging that creeps do to noncreeps. This was the type of bugging that only best friends can do to best friends. This was the type of bugging that comes from being so comfortable around each other that you can say or be anything you want . . . even if you're not always as polite as you should be.

Today they were haggling over baseball cards.

"Listen," Louis said nervously. Both boys were peering over their cards at each other as intently as a couple of poker players in an old Western. But by the look on Louis's face the "game" wasn't going as well as he had hoped. Apparently Nicholas had the upper hand. "I'll uh . . . I'll give you Guerrero, Robin Yount, and, uh . . . ," Louis hesitated a moment. Now it was getting crucial. One false move and he could blow the whole deal. "Uh . . . Ricky Henderson!" he finished with a nervous smile. "You can't beat that!"

Nicholas grinned. You couldn't fool him. He had Louis on the ropes and he knew it. Now it was time to go in for the kill. "You'll have to do better than that, Bucko, if you want Will Clark's *rookie* card!"

"Oh, man," Louis groaned.

Now it's true, these were just baseball cards. But to the guys it couldn't get any more tense than if they were dealing stock on Wall Street.

"Listen, Louis," Nicholas said trying to console him (after all, they were good friends). "That's a decent offer and stuff. But I'm not interested in parting with Will Clark. Not at any price. *No reason. No how. No way!*"

Suddenly Thurman's meaty paw appeared and neatly plucked the Will Clark card out of Nick's deck. "All right!" he exclaimed as he plopped down beside them. "A present for me?"

"Hey, big guy," Nicholas said without a blink, "he's all yours." He threw a glance over to Louis who was so impressed with Nick's cowardice that he accidentally broke the plastic spoon off in his mouth.

"Thanks," Thurman grinned as he nonchalantly folded and crammed the precious card into his pocket. The boys' mouths dropped open. If thoughts could be heard, their anguished cries would have shattered every window in the shop: "That's Will Clark he's demolishing!"

"Hey, how 'bout that last pitch?" Thurman laughed.

At first the guys didn't hear—either because of all the ice cream in Thurman's mouth or because they were still staring at the little lump of what used to be a baseball card stuffed in the big fellow's pocket.

In any case, Thurman didn't notice. He just kept right on eating and right on talking. "No way I'm gonna let that bozo get a fastball by me," he continued to laugh, his mouth full of strawberries, blueberries, Oreo chips, pralines, caramel sauce, chocolate sprinkles, and a dab of Raspberry Ripple ice cream. Not a pretty sight.

But somehow Nick was able to force a grin. "You said it!" he agreed, putting on his best I'm-going-to-pretend-I-like-this-guy-even-though-he-just-ripped-off-my-favorite-baseball-card grin. "No way. Right, Louis?"

Louis was still staring at the wadded lump in Thurman's pocket.

"Yo, Louis?" Nick repeated.

"No way . . . no how . . . ," Louis mumbled, still staring at the pocket.

"Hey!" Thurman shouted angrily.

Suddenly Louis snapped back to reality. But Thurman wasn't yelling at him. He was staring at his ice cream.

"She forgot my walnuts!" he growled.

Both boys watched with fascination as Thurman rose to his feet and lumbered back toward the counter. What few Braves there were still in line stepped aside as he approached. They'd waited this long for some ice cream, a little longer wouldn't hurt. In fact, by the look on Thurman's face, it might actually prove to be healthier to wait.

"Hey," another voice called. "Get a load of the All-Stars!"

Nicholas gave a little shudder. He immediately recognized the voice. It belonged to one of Derrick's dorks. And where his dorks were, Derrick Cryder, the all-school bad guy, was soon to follow. Maybe if Nick kept his back to him, Derrick wouldn't notice he was there. Maybe if Nick covered the side of his face with his hand. Maybe if—

"Hey, Martin!" Derrick shouted at him from across the room.

Then again, maybe not.

"What's with these outfits?" the bully jeered as he sauntered toward him. "Your Girl Scout troop on a field trip?"

"Lay off, Cryder," Nick said, trying his best to sound tough. Ever since he had beaten Derrick in the skateboard race, Nicholas knew that the guy really respected him, deep down inside—deep, *deep* down inside. The only problem was that it was so deep the guy didn't know it yet. So Nicholas would call his bluff by sounding cool and in control.

"We happen to be celebrating," he said in his most casual tone of voice. "We're the new city champs."

"You mean 'city *chumps*,'" Derrick sneered as he reached out and grabbed Nick's hat.

So much for bluffing.

"Hey, is this hat full of mush . . . like your head?" It was a stupid joke, but because Derrick Cryder made it, Derrick Cryder laughed at it. And because Derrick Cryder laughed at it, so did his dorks. That was the price of dorkhood.

"Knock it off, Derrick!" Nicholas protested. "And give me my hat." Nick tried to grab it, but his size and height were no match for the bigger kid.

"Oh, yeah," Derrick taunted. "You and whose army?" Once again his comeback wasn't all that funny. In fact, it didn't even make that much sense. But once again the dorks gave the required laugh. That is until a mammoth hand suddenly reached over and grabbed Derrick Cryder's left earlobe.

"YEOWWWWWW!!!" Derrick screamed.

All eyes followed the mammoth hand up to the

mammoth arm, up to the mammoth chest of, you
guessed it . . . Thurman Miller.

"Nice earring," Thurman grinned as he fingered
the golden stud in Derrick's lobe.

"Let go, let go!" Derrick demanded. He tried to
squirm, to see who dared touch his prized posses-
sion, but one twist of Thurman's hand put a stop
to that in a hurry. A big hurry.

"OOOWWWWWWW!"

"I bet it'd hurt real bad if you lost this earring,"
Thurman said, thinking out loud.

Again Derrick tried to get a look and again Thurman froze him in his tracks with another tug.

"OOOOOOOOO!" Derrick cried.

"It's real pretty, too," Thurman smiled. "My little
sister has one just like it."

By now Derrick had learned his lesson. He wasn't moving a muscle.

Finally, after Thurman was sure he had made his point, he very gently and oh, so politely growled, "You wanna give back the hat now?"

"OK, OK, OK," Derrick cried as he quickly tossed the hat back to Nicholas.

At last Thurman released his ear, with just a little tweak and twist tossed in for good measure.

Quickly Derrick spun around, ready to destroy whoever had humiliated him . . . that is until he saw Thurman. Well, actually, to be more specific, until he saw Thurman's muscles. Thurman's muscles and his smile. A smile that was quickly turning to a frown.

Suddenly, for the first time in his life, Derrick Cryder knew fear.

"Beat it," Thurman scowled.

And beat it Derrick did—in a hurry . . . a big hurry, with his dorks quickly following after him.

Nick and Louis looked on with awe. Watching Thurman handle Derrick was like watching a master artist at work. But the big guy paid little attention. Instead he plopped down like nothing had happened—like traumatizing the town terror was just part of his daily routine.

An instant later Thurman's scowl returned. "One of you guys wanna get me a napkin?" he asked as he looked to the boys.

"I'll get it," Nick said as he jumped from his chair.

"Let me," Louis argued.

"I got it," Nick insisted.

Now it was a race to see who would be the first to the counter and back again with the prized napkin for their brand-new protector and all-around idol. . . .

Mom poured Dad a cup of coffee as the kids cleared the dinner dishes from the table. All the time they were eating Nick had gone on and on about Thurman Miller. He talked about him through Grandma's pork chops, sauerkraut, and potatoes. And he talked about him through little Jamie's failed attempt at dessert—strawberry Jell-O with whipped cream. The whipped cream part came out OK. But something went haywire with the Jell-O. So instead of enjoying nice jiggly strawberry Jell-O, everyone was enjoying nice slurpy strawberry soup. Of course, no one mentioned it to Jamie. After all, she was only in second grade and they didn't want to give her some sort of anti-cooking complex.

"He'll probably be signed right out of high school," Nick continued as he scooped the glasses up and headed for the sink, "with a major league contract for a million dollars!"

"OK!" Sarah sighed her world-famous big sister sigh. "Enough about Thurman *Munster*, already!"

"That's Miller, not Munster," Nick corrected.

"I call 'em like I see 'em," she snipped.

"All right, you two," Dad interrupted. Like any good dad he knew when an argument was about to break out. And like any good dad he wasn't in the mood for listening to one. Still, he felt Nick had a good point about Thurman's talents. "The kid is amazing," he confessed to Mom. "No one can deny that. Nick's probably right about the pros, too. Thurman's definitely major league material."

By now Sarah was at the sink. Try as she might, she couldn't resist the temptation of banging the plates down just a little too hard on the counter . . . then scrapping them just a little too vigorously. "Oh, yes," she sighed dreamily. "And just think, the next step is *real* greatness . . . when they name a candy bar after him!"

Nicholas completely missed the sarcasm. Instead, for the first time in his life, he actually agreed with his sister. "Hey, you're right!" he exclaimed. "Like 'Miller Munchies' or . . . or 'Thurman Thingles.'"

"Thurman Thingles!" Sarah groaned in her best how-can-I-live-with-such-a-hopeless-case-for-a-little-brother voice.

But before Nick could respond, the phone rang.

"Hello?" Mom answered. "Oh, sure. Hang on." She held the phone out to Dad with a half smile. "It's for you . . . Coach."

A puzzled look crossed Dad's face as he reached for the phone. "Hello?" The puzzled look quickly turned into a depressed look. "Oh, hi, Harvey."

"Who's that, Mom?" Sarah asked.

Mom shook her head in amusement and answered, "Let's just say it ain't Publisher's Clearing House."

"What? You're kidding." Suddenly Dad's voice took on an even gloomier tone. He removed the receiver from his ear so the rest of the family could hear the snorts of laughter coming from the other end. They were so loud and obnoxious they could

LIBRARY
DEXTER SCHOOLS
DEXTER NM 88230

almost have come from Arnold the Pig instead of Harvey the whomever.

The family glanced at one another in amazement. What on earth . . . ?

"Oh, sure." Dad was back on the phone. "I can hardly wait—it'll be like old times." He rolled his eyes as more snorting came through the receiver. Then finally he brought the conversation to an end. "Right . . . see you next week." With that, he hung up and finished his sentence, "You big bag of wind."

"David . . . ," Mom admonished lightly.

"Well, of all the crummy breaks," Dad grumbled.

"Who was that?" little Jamie asked.

"Harvey Stover," Dad grumbled, "the biggest blowhard in the league. He's managing the team we're playing in the regionals."

"So?" asked Nick.

"So-o?" Dad looked at him with surprise. "You've got a short memory, son. His team knocked us out of the playoffs last year!"

"Oh, of course!" Nick said, finally catching on. "The guy who snorts!"

"Bingo," Dad answered. Then suddenly his voice got very low and very serious. "Well, I promise you one thing. Not this year! Things are going to be different this time around, ol' Harvey-boy!"

Mom threw a nervous glance in his direction. Dad . . . Mr. Level-Headed, Mr. Always-in-Control . . . Mr. Spiritual-Leader-of-the-Home . . . was having a problem. It didn't happen often. But, once in a while, it happened. It probably had something to do with his being human.

"No sir, buddy-boy," he muttered, growing more

serious. "This year I get even. This year it's payback time." With that he grabbed his fork and jabbed it squarely into the last piece of cantaloupe. "Yes sir," he continued, "this year we've got Thurman Miller!" He plopped the cantaloupe into his mouth and chewed with relish.

Nick, who was caught up in his father's spell of victory, couldn't help breaking into a big grin.

Mom, on the other hand, was not grinning. Somehow she sensed that things were going to get a little sticky around the old homestead. Somehow she knew that some attitudes weren't entirely right. And that meant that maybe, just maybe, the Lord would be stepping in to do a little attitude adjustment. . . .

FOUR
"I Don't Care if I Ever Get Back . . . "

The crowd gasped as I entered the arena and saun-tered toward the weight-lifting platform. Up until now they had only read of my amazing strength (and incredibly manicured pinkies), but now, at last, they were able to see it. I bulged my biceps, tried my triceps, and toided my deltoids. Young women were swooning. Young men were green with envy.

And why not? After all, it was I, The Regrettable Bulk . . . world-famous wrestler and soon-to-be Weight-Lifting Champion of the World!

I glanced up to the platform. My arch rival, Nick the Hick, that towering, two-ton terror from Tennes-see, was about to tout some tremendous tonnage.

A hush fell over the crowd as he reached down to the barbell. For a moment he hesitated. Obviously the kid was dreaming of all that prize money. Money that would fulfill his wildest dreams . . . cars, houses, all the CDs he could fit in his spa-

cious, state-of-the-art rec room. Money that, if he was lucky, just might cover most of his chiropractic bills.

For months we'd been training for this one event. The Hick with all of his farm activities . . . you know, like bailing hay, chopping cotton, bench pressing tractors. And me with my excruciatingly intensive workouts of watching MTV, Nickelodeon, and—when I was feeling exceptionally strong—slipping in a little Mr. Rogers.

Then of course there were our diets. The Hick had his special meals of organically grown vegetables, farm-fresh fruit, and whole goat's milk. I, on the other hand, disciplined myself by eating all the junk food from chapter 1.

Now at last we were ready. With an earth-shattering cry, the Hick hoisted the barbell to his waist. The crowd ooohed. Then with a mighty shout he pushed it high over his head before leaping out of the way and letting it crash back to the platform.

The crowd was on its feet clapping and cheering wildly. Some were even throwing roses. I showed my enthusiasm by trying to stifle a yawn. Sure, he had just set a new record by pressing over 2000 pounds. But hey, what's a ton or two between such sinuous superstars as ourselves? The contest wasn't over. Not by a long shot.

Now it was my turn. Without a moment's hesitation I strutted onto the stage. Quickly I reached down and placed my hands on the long bar of the barbell, and with a mighty shout tried to lift it. It wouldn't budge. I tried again. Hey, what's the big idea—somebody bolt this to the stage or somethin'?

First the audience began to snicker. Then they began to laugh. Then they began to hoot. . . . Then boo. I glanced down at my hands. Wait a minute! This was no barbell I was trying to lift! This was one of the roses they had thrown on the stage.

I gave one last heave-ho but with no luck. So the audience decided to give the heave-ho a try, too—with me. "Get him off!" they shouted. "We want our money back!"

In its fury, the crowd began to climb onto the stage and race toward me. Now don't get me wrong. I love adoring fans as much as the next incredible (and perfectly manicured) superstar. But these guys looked like they were after more than just my autograph.

I turned and started to run, but they were coming at me from all sides.

"Nicholas!" I shouted. "Nicholas get me out of here!"

"McGee!" I could hear my little buddy's voice but I couldn't see him.

"NICHOLAS!"

"McGee . . . McGee, snap out of it. McGEE!"

Suddenly I was back in Nick's bedroom. The arena had dissolved and so had my adoring fans. What a pity, and we were getting to be such close friends, too.

"You were having another daydream," Nicholas said between grunts. He was working out on his weight machine.

"More like a day-mare," I said with a shudder.

Nick gave a smirk as he continued his workout. Mind you, this wasn't just any weight machine.

This was your Handy-Dandy-Homemade-with-a-Pile-of-Encyclopedias-Tied-Together-with-Ropes-that-Lead-to-Pulleys-in-the-Ceiling-and-Come-Back-Down weight machine. One of our better inventions, if I do say so myself.

Yes-siree-bob, I was back in reality, sitting at my own weight machine, where for several minutes I had been suffering, agonizing, and worst of all, actually sweating. That's right, I'm not ashamed to admit it. I'd actually begun to work up a dew on my incredible, manly brow. Sweat—what an awful invention. Worse than veggie burgers or even turkey hot dogs. OK, well, maybe not that bad, but not a lot of fun—especially when you're a cartoon character painted with watercolors that run when they get damp.

Anyways, Nick and I kept pulling on the weights, again and again . . . and again some more.

"Ghuuuh," I groaned as I gave another tug. "Refresh my memory. What's the point of all this?"

"Strength," Nick gasped between pulls. "If you're strong, you can't lose. Just look at Thurman. He hit that homer today because of all the power in his forearms."

"Four arms," I groaned. "No wonder I can't lift this thing. I've only got two arms!" I tried one last pull, but it was more than I could handle. Before I knew it the weights went crashing down. Unfortunately, I forgot to let go. So as the weights went crashing down, my arms went shooting up . . . stretching like a wad of Silly Putty on a hot summer day.

"See how the training helps?" Nick said with a snicker. "You're already improving your reach."

I began rolling in my arms like giant garden hoses. "Ho-ho," I sneered, "that's rich." But before I could hit him with one of my world-class, Triple-A, snappy comebacks, Dad opened the door.

"Well," he said grinning one of his famous fatherly grins. "How's the weight training coming?"

"Oh, hi Dad," Nick answered as he glanced around to make sure I was out of sight. "I'm just taking a little break."

"Good idea," Mr. Dad nodded. "You gotta take it easy when you first get started." By now he had moved in for a closer look at our incredible, do-it-yourself weight machine. "That's quite a contraption you've got there."

Good ol' Mr. Dad. He'd seen all of our inventions . . . the Hydro-Powered Pencil Sharpener, the Jet-Powered Alarm Clock, the Remote-Control Clothes Dryer, and our infamous Make-You-Think-We're-in-the-Room-When-We're-Really-Out-Catching-a-Flick-We-Shouldn't-Be-Catching Answering Machine. But no matter what the invention, he always played it cool and pretended they were just something you'd expect from your average, run-of-the-mill, intellectual genius types.

"Thanks." Nick nodded as he accepted the compliment. "Of course, Thurman has a real weight machine at his house." Good ol' Nick. As an official kid he knows the value of throwing in a little guilt to make his parents feel he's deprived. It never hurts to build up those guilt reserves for future causes.

"I'm not surprised," Mr. Dad said, neatly sidestepping the guilt trap. "Guys like Thurman always set a winning example. Hey," he added as he crawled underneath the bar and cords of the weight machine. "Put another couple of books on this thing."

"Sure," Nick agreed.

As Dad finished sliding into place, Nick grabbed volumes L and M of the encyclopedias to throw on the machine.

"You know, Nick, this ball game really means a lot to me," he said. Then, suddenly remembering he was a parent and above such childish desires as wanting to stomp Harvey the Snorter, Dad started over. "Er, that is, this ball game means a lot to all of us." He motioned for Nicholas to toss the N and O-P volumes onto the weight pile, too. "In a game like this," he continued, "everybody's got to pull their weight to win."

Nick nodded as he plopped the volumes onto the pile, which was getting bigger by the second. Dad glanced at the pile, then motioned to Nick. "Go ahead," he insisted. "I can handle more than that." Dad was obviously in one of his more macho moods.

Nicholas gave the pile a dubious look. Then, after a shrug, grabbed Q-R, S and T, and tossed them onto the pile as well.

At last Mr. Dad gave the bar a pull.

Nothing.

He pulled the bar a little harder.

Repeat performance. The weights wouldn't budge. He cleared his throat, frowned in concentration, and tried again.

Same results. Nothing moved—not a fraction.

Most Dads would have been pretty embarrassed

by now. But always in charge, and always the one to set the good example, Mr. Dad quickly changed the subject. "Well, this has been fun, but I'd better get going. Things are pretty hectic right now, so I'm really too busy to lift weights." It was an old ploy, one of the first they teach you in Dad School, and he pulled it off like a pro. "But don't worry, I'll, uh, I'll help you with your weights some other time."

For a moment Nick was confused then he broke into a smile. He knew exactly what was going on. "Sure, Dad," he grinned.

"Anyway, what I was trying to say about the game," Mr. Dad continued as he attempted to climb out of the machine (somehow getting in was a lot easier than getting out), "what I was trying to say is that you and the other guys need to turn it up a notch. Thurman's got to have support on the mound, so I need you to give it all you have this week, OK?"

"Right, Dad."

Still struggling to untangle himself from the bar and cords, Dad nodded and added, "The other guys, too."

"Sure, Dad."

More struggling. "I mean I really want to win this one."

"Absolutely, Dad."

Finally, just when Nick was starting to wonder if he'd have to step in and give his dad a hand, Mr. Dad managed to untangle himself and get out. His hair looked like he was doing an Einstein imitation, and his clothes were all cockeyed, but he still managed to look down to Nick with a fatherly, I-know-exactly-what-I'm-doing grin. "That's great, son," he said, patting Nick on the shoulder. "I knew you'd understand."

Nick tried not to smile.

Then with one last pat and a little hair tousling thrown in for good measure, Mr. Dad turned and headed out of the room, all the time trying to rub out the aches that had suddenly appeared in his shoulders.

Nicholas looked after him, smiling. He loved his dad. And he respected him . . . weaknesses and all.

FIVE
"'Cause It's Root, Root, Root for the Home Team . . ."

The following day, everybody got up nice and early to get to practice. And I do mean *early*. In fact, Nick got up so early that for the first time in his life he was able to get into the bathroom before his sisters. It was a strange sensation seeing an absolutely spotless counter—no eyeliners, eyeshadows, or lipsticks scattered across its surface. There wasn't even the usual array of rouge, baby powder, hair dryers, and electric curlers. It was even stranger not having to scrape off the layer of hair spray that normally collected on the mirror during Sarah's multiple coats of hair varnish. Strangest of all was not having his nose twitch and itch over the nauseating aromas of bath oils, shampoos, and perfumes.

The sun was just peeking over the trees as the bleary-eyed team stumbled onto the field for a torturous workout. It wasn't that Dad was interested in winning or anything like that. He just wanted to make sure that there was absolutely no way in heaven or on earth, by accident or on purpose, on land or sea, by gosh or by golly, that Harvey the Snorter's team would come anywhere close to beating them again.

"All right, everybody," Dad clapped as he cheered the kids onto the field. "Heads up, look alive now."

The kids looked anything but "alive" as they staggered toward their positions. Everyone was still groggy and half-asleep. Well, almost everyone.

Thurman Miller had been up for hours. He had to be to squeeze in his weight lifting, his four-mile run, and his three glasses of Macho-Muscle Protein Drink.

"Right, Coach!" he bellowed as he dropped down to do a dozen squat thrusts for warm-up.

Nicholas and Louis stared. Amazing. This was their hero. This was the guy they dreamed of imitating—and he was doing warm-ups in the middle of the night without even being asked! Crazy. Absurd. Loony Tunes. So Loony Tunes that Nicholas and Louis glanced at each other and, without a word, dropped down to join him. What other choice did they have?

A little later, Thurman, all decked out with wristbands, a batting glove, and a billion pieces of Big Chew bubble gum stuffed into his cheek, stepped up to the plate. He gave a few practice swings and calmly waited to start bashing the ball out of the park.

Off to the side, Nicholas and Louis were also putting on their wrist bands and batting gloves (which just happened to be the same style and color as Thurman's).

"The left hand," Nicholas whispered.

Louis looked up. "Huh?"

"The left hand. Your batting glove goes on the *left* hand."

Louis shot a look over to Thurman. Nick was right. Their hero was wearing it on his left hand. Quickly the boy changed hands.

"Got any Big Chew?" Nicholas asked.

"Naw," Louis shrugged as he pulled the empty pouch from his pocket. "I gave the last of it to Thurman."

For a moment Nick was lost. How could he be like Thurman Miller if he didn't have any Big Chew? If Thurman Miller had Big Chew then Nicholas Martin would need Big Chew. It was a simple fact.

Finally a simple solution came to mind. Without a second thought, Nicholas wadded up the empty pouch, popped it into his mouth and stuffed it into one of his cheeks. Now he looked just like Thurman Miller. It was a brilliant idea. At least until he noticed the taste. Then he couldn't spit the pouch out fast enough.

"Cool," Louis smirked as Nick continued to cough and spit. "Real cool."

"Hey, you guys!" Thurman called.

Immediately both boys spun around.

"Hit the outfield for some flies!"

Say no more. His wish was their command. They grabbed their gloves and raced toward the field.

Meanwhile, Dad was concentrating on the statistics on his clipboard. All yesterday evening he had been working up strategies. All night he had been dreaming about them. All day today he would be working them out. It wasn't an easy job, but it was one of the many things that had to be done to make sure Harvey the Snorter didn't stand a chance of winning.

Suddenly there were three loud snorts followed by obnoxious laughter. Dad cringed. He knew what would happen next. And, sure enough, just like clockwork, Harvey the Snorter's big clumsy hand crashed down on Dad's shoulder . . . a little too hard and a little too friendly. "Hey, Dave!" the big man shouted just a little too loudly. "How's the *second* best manager in the League?"

"Fine, just fine," Dad said, doing his best imitation of a smile, which ended up being more grimace than grin. "Good to see you, Harvey." OK, so it wasn't exactly the truth, but Dad didn't want to hurt the big guy's feelings. Then, out of the corner of his eye, Dad noticed Thurman smashing the ball to the fielders. Come to think of it, maybe he *was* telling the truth . . . maybe he *was* glad to see Harvey.

Harvey snorted again as he gave Dad another big slap on the back. "You know, Dave, considering last year's massacre, no one would blame you if you forfeited the game this Saturday." He broke out with a wheezy laugh. "I mean, you'd sure save us all a lot of trouble." He ended with a couple more snorts.

Once again Thurman laid into the ball. And

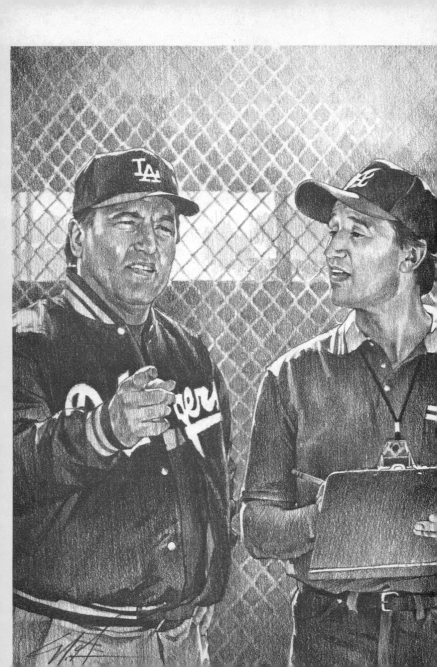

once again Nicholas and Louis watched as it sailed high over their heads and of the park.

This time Harvey noticed it, too. "Hey, nice hitting. Who's your assistant?"

It was Dad's turn to grin. No grimace this time. It was a real, legitimate grin. "That's Thurman Miller. . ." He hesitated a second, savoring the moment. Then finally he finished, "my *pitcher.*"

"Your WHAT!?"

Thurman smashed another ball, and it sailed high over Nick's head and out of the park. Thurman had cost the team a fortune in baseballs, but right now Dad figured it was worth every penny.

Harvey the Snorter watched in stunned amazement.

"What's the matter, Harv?" Dad teased. "You look kinda pale."

Harvey the Snorter tried to answer but he could only stare as Thurman prepared to hit another ball.

Dad continued the dig. "I hope you're not coming down with anything. You know, like *chicken* pox . . ."

Thurman smacked another.

At last Harvey the Snorter was able to speak as he fumbled for his glasses. "Whattaya trying to pull, Martin?" he sputtered, slipping on the spectacles for a better look. "That guy played Triple-A for the Cubs last season! I'm sure of it!"

Dad's grin was looking more and more like the Cheshire cat's. "He's thirteen years old," he gloated. "And he meets all the Little League requirements. What else do you want to know, Sherlock?"

Thurman clobbered another one out of the park.

By now, Harvey was no longer snorting. Instead he was starting to stutter. "You, you wantta get ugly?" he finally managed to blurt out. "I . . . I can get ugly."

"I'll bet you can," Dad agreed.

"I've got a few surprises, too, Martin. We'll see who has the last laugh—just like last year!"

"Last year is history, pal. Just like your winning streak."

"Oh . . . oh, yeah?" Harvey the Snorter demanded.

"Catchy comeback, Harv. We'll see you Saturday." With that, Dad dismissed the man and turned to watch Thurman clobber another ball out of the park.

Harvey the Snorter would have stuck around to watch, but he had other things to do—like storm to his car, like drive to the nearest Golden Arches, and like eat himself into oblivion—something the man always did when he was upset. And today he was real upset: three Big Macs, two sides of fries, and four chocolate shakes' worth of upset.

Meanwhile, Nicholas and Louis were still out in the field watching balls sail over their heads.

"See that cloud, there?" Nick asked. "It's kinda shaped like the trophy we're gonna win at the Regionals. . . ."

But Louis wasn't watching the clouds, he was watching another Thurman Miller Special shoot high into orbit. "Man, how'd you like to be able to hit like that?"

Still staring at the clouds, Nicholas nodded. Although his eyes were on the clouds, his mind was already a million miles away, experiencing another world-famous Nicholas Martin fantasy. . . .

"Next up," the announcer's voice reverberated about the stadium. "It's Slam-the-Man Martin, the greatest home run hitter of all time!"

Immediately the crowd of 1.3 million spectators (hey, it's Nick's fantasy, he can have as many people as he wants) was on its feet cheering. Next it began to chant: "Mar-tin! Mar-tin! Mar-tin!"

Finally, the mighty Slam Martin stepped out of the dugout. A tremendous roar filled the stadium. Strangely enough, Slam-the-Man was decked out exactly like Thurman Miller, to the very last detail. Of course, the muscles looked a little phony but it was the best Nick could dream up on such short notice. This time he had some real Big Chew in his mouth. Yes sir, no fooling around now. Slam Martin was ready to be a world-famous hero . . . again.

He gave a wink to the TV cameras, waved to the President and First Lady, then strolled toward the plate. The bases were loaded. All they needed was one little ol' grand slam and they would win. By now the roar was deafening as Slam took a couple practice swings and waited.

For a moment he felt a twinge of pity for the pitcher. It was Orel Hershiser. Poor guy. He may be the greatest pitcher known to man, but his great greatness was no match for the greatness of the great Slam Martin.

Orel knew it, too. I mean the guy was sweating like a Sumo wrestler in a sauna. Obviously he knew he didn't stand a chance—mainly because he knew whose daydream this was. But he had no choice—he had to go through with the game. Finally he took a deep breath and began the windup.

Slam crouched low and waited.

Orel fired the ball. It was the best pitch of his life. The crowd gasped in awe, but you could barely hear them over the sonic boom the ball made as it broke the sound barrier and rocketed toward Martin.

But Slam wasn't worried. In fact, he did his best to stifle a yawn as the super-sonic projectile hurtled toward him at a zillion miles an hour. At first Slam wasn't sure what to do: did he want to hit a home run or just a triple? After all, he liked Orel and didn't want to embarrass the guy too much. Then he remembered that the fate of the entire free world rested on this one pitch. (Apparently our president and the secretary general of the Soviet Union had a little bet riding on the game. Something about a title deed to North America. . . .)

So Slam Martin leaned back and swung.

K-THWAK!

The ball sailed high, higher, and even higher until it was completely out of sight. In fact, it sailed so high that one of the umpires had to go in and call air traffic control just to keep track of it on radar. The crowd was going crazy as Slam trotted around the bases and followed the other runners home. Everyone raced onto the field, hoisted him to their shoulders, then carried him into the locker room to celebrate.

Everything was going perfect. Well, almost everything. There was one little catch. No one had really figured that the ball would hit the bottom of a high-flying 747 and bounce directly back into the park. But, of course, that's exactly what happened. Before Slam and the other runners were able to get out of the locker room and back onto their bases, the center fielder caught the returning ball and fired it around the infield for a triple play.

The crowd booed. Then it hissed. Then it booed and hissed.

The great Slam Martin hung his head in shame. Why had he been so careless, so overconfident? A real pro would have expected something like that to happen.

"Don't feel too bad, Slam." The boy looked up. It was Orel walking beside him, putting his arm around him. "There's more to life than winning. Besides, no single player can expect to do it all. It takes a whole team to win a game."

Suddenly Orel's voice began to sound sneakingly familiar . . . and suddenly Nick's daydream began to dissolve. He was back in the Little League field watching a fly ball finish rolling to a stop at his feet.

"Come on, it takes a whole team to win a game!" It was Dad shouting. "Let's wake up out there! Come on now, we have a long way to go!"

Well, so much for another sensational Nicholas Martin daydream.

But Dad was right. They did have a long way to go. Longer than either father or son could imagine. . . .

SIX
"If They Don't Win It's a Shame . . . "

Yes-siree-bob, ol' Nicky-boy and his pop were pretty serious about winning. Too serious, if you ask me. It's like I always say, "It's not whether you win or lose that counts, it's how bad Thurman demolishes your opponent." No, no, no, that's what they've been saying. What I say is, "It's not whether you win or lose that counts, it's who gets to eat all the popcorn and hot dogs left over after the concession stand closes." Well, that's not exactly right either . . . but I think you get the picture.

Of course, what I really wanted was for my little buddy to see what was really happening—to understand that he was putting too much stock in Thurman. And I was kinda curious where he thought God fit into all of this . . . assuming he'd thought about God at all lately. But hey, I had more important things to do than throw these questions at my buddy. . . like getting my hands on his Ryne Sandberg baseball card!

We were up in his room, and I had just offered him my favorite Slimy Cleavus card. You know Slimy, the world-famous cartoon outfielder and part-time used-car salesman? It was my best offer, but Nick just wasn't biting.

"Who's this guy supposed to be?" he demanded.

"Who's he supposed to be?! Are you kidding? Slimy is headed for the Hall of Fame!"

"Right," Nicholas scoffed. "The Geek Hall of Fame."

I was obviously ringing up a No Sale with Nick, so it was time to put all my cards on the table . . . literally.

"All right," I said as I fanned the rest of my baseball cards out onto his bed. "I'll even throw in Oxo Nubbins."

Nick just looked at me. Man! Talk about driving a hard bargain.

"OK, OK, how 'bout Slats Felldoe?"

"Slats Felldoe?" he asked incredulously. It was pretty obvious he didn't know much about the National Cartoon League.

"OK, kid, tell ya what I'm gonna do. In trade for your Ryne Sandberg, you can be the proud owner of Slimy Cleavus and Otho Mounds . . . a legend in his own grime!"

"McGee," he said with a sigh.

All right! He was finally starting to weaken. He was finally starting to see reason. He was finally starting to—

"Get a brain, will ya?"

—get on my nerves. I had no choice. He left me no alternative. Now it was time to mesmerize him with my marvelously magnificent McGeeisms. I grabbed a nearby pencil and took a few practice swings. "I tell you, Buddy-Boy, that Cleavus had one mean swing." I pulled an imaginary ball from my back pocket, the one I keep there for just such occasions. Tossing it into the air, I did my best Cleavus swing and smacked that sphere to Saturn. Well, almost . . .

First it got Nick's lamp—ZING!

Then it decked his dinosaur—ZONG!

Then it nailed the world globe—ZANG!

Then it ricocheted off the mirror—ZUNG!

Then it clobbered me on the bean—OUCH!

Suddenly the room was full of stars . . . and we ain't talkin' Sylvester or Madonna, here. I staggered this way and that, that way and this. Then I felt this strange urge to lie down. It wasn't like I was tired or anything like that, but I'd heard it's the in thing to do when you're knocked unconscious. And, not wanting to be out of style, I followed suit. . . .

CRASH-BOOM!

Fortunately Nick was right there at my side. As usual, he tried to help me with his gentle kindness, his tender concern, and his quiet words of encouragement: "I hope you have baseball out of your system now, Pine Tar Breath!"

His gentle bedside manner was all it took. Immediately I was back on my feet. "Are you kidding?" I argued. "And give up all that fame and fortune?" Already I could hear the clanking of change, the grabbing of greenbacks, the swishing of savings certificates. "Big leagues mean big bucks," I insisted. "Just in endorsements alone!"

To prove my point, I let go with a lightning- like

leap landing me lightly on the lad's lap. (Say that three times fast.) Nick grabbed his pencil, reached for his sketch pad, and let me hop onto the paper. Then, before you could say, "Uh-oh, here comes another fantasy," I was starring in one of those super-jock commercials.

Hmm, looks like I'm in some old black-and-white newsreel footage. It's back in my "good ol' days," when I was playing center field for the New York Hankies. And what's old black-and-white footage without some old-time, play-by-play announcing?

"Ladies and gentlemen, you should hear the roar of this crowd out here in Mile Sty Stadium. Slugger Stan Steroid steps to the plate. There's the wind-up, the pitch and . . . the Steroid slams another one toward center field!

"Center fielder McGee drops back . . . back . . . this one may be out of here folks! Now McGee's on the warning track, now he jumps and . . . what a sensational catch! McGee leaps high over the fence, stealing a homer and the winning run from the Steroid Kid! Just listen to this crowd!"

Suddenly, we're pulling back from the TV monitor and there I am again, only thirty years later. Man alive, what a bod, what a face, and what terrific acting. Just listen. . . .

"Yes sir, that was . . . uh, I mean, that was me, yeah me, back in . . . don't tell me, oh yeah, 1962. Pretty impressive, huh? But these, uh, I mean . . . that is to say, these days I call the, uh, the big plays, uh, behind the mike in the, what do you call it, oh yeah, the press box and, uh, er, uh, I . . ."

OK, OK, I know I sound a little stiff, but I get better. Just keep watching.

"And, after uh, oh yeah, after a hard day . . . phew . . . I like to freshen up with a little, a little splash of Old Lice After-Shave."

Pretty good job, huh? And look what a great job I'm doing of holding the bottle up to the camera. And look how fast I'm turning it around so it's right side up. What a pro. Shhh . . . I've got one more line.

"Yes sir! Get some Old Lice . . . for the louse in your life!"

I glanced up at Nick from the sketch pad. "What do you think, kiddo?"

"Nah," Nick said as he ripped out the page and started drawing again. . . .

Oh, hey, this is even better. Now I'm lounging around the pool. There must be a thousand-and-one beautiful gals hanging around. Obviously just a small cross-section of my many adoring fans. Oh, wait, I'm getting ready to speak. . . .

"Ya know, these days when I work up a big thirst, I like to quench it with an ice-cold Canine Cola."

All right! Check out the big grin I'm giving to the camera as I'm reaching past the bag of Ava's Pork Rinds to the can which, of course, has a picture of a big dog on it. Now I'm chugging it down, and instead of a burp out comes a mighty "WOOF!!"

Then of course, I have to give the little wink to the camera. And let's not forget the ever-popular jingle. Talk about original!

"Drink Canine Cola, la-la-la . . .
it's doggone good. WOOF!"

Wow! What a masterpiece! What perfection. Look out, Academy Awards, here I come.

I threw a glance up to Nicholas to congratulate him on a job well-done, but the kid wasn't smiling. Apparently he still felt it wasn't quite right.

Artists—who can figure 'em?

He ripped out the page and tried for one last commercial . . .

Ahhh, this is more like it. I'm in my rugged outdoorsman uniform. You know, the one with the plaid shirt, cuffed jeans, and the ever-popular, steel-toed logging boots. And speaking of logging, that's me cutting down that tree. My oh my, look how I swing that ax . . .

SCHUNK! . . . SCHUNK! . . . SCHUNK!

Now I'm dusting the manly dust from my manly hands, and looking at the camera and giving my marvelously manly smile. As I start walking toward my new pickup I begin to talk. . . .

"Y'know, when I played ball, it was a tough game. But not as tough as the payments on my new Shimmy Truck."

I give the ol' Shimmy a pat on the side before climbing in.

Now we cut to the next scene, and I'm heading down a steep mountain road, the truck bouncing and shimmying like Jell-O on a jackhammer. I try to talk but the vibrations are pretty strong. . . .

"A-n-d-d-d y-y-y-ou t-t-t-alk-k-k a-b-a-b-out t-t-t-ough . . ."

I seem to be picking up too much speed, so I try the brakes. Funny, they don't seem to be working as well as they should. Come to think of it, they're not working at all! But that's OK, I'm a professional. I can still say my lines. . . .

"Y-y-y-ou ough-t-t-t to s-s-s-ee the wa-ay-ay-ay this b-b-b-ab-b-b-y hand-d-d-dles."

Things are starting to get serious. I'm going so fast that the trees on one side are a blur. If I hit any of them it could really smart—not to mention mess up my fabulously combed hair. Fortunately there are no trees on the other side. Just a 358-foot drop-off.

A 358-FOOT DROP-OFF?!

OK, OK, that's no problem for a cool, in-control superstar athlete like myself. I'll just downshift. I'll just take this old gearshift here and . . .

GRIND! GRIND! GRIND!

Hmm, must be something wrong with the clutch. Maybe if I just pump it a little. . . .

PUMP! PUMP! PUMP!

Uh-oh . . .

GRIND! GRIND! GRIND!

PUMP! PUMP! PUMP!

Did you ever have one of those days?

Faster and faster I race down the road. But never being one to lose my head—I clear my throat and calmly scream:

"N I C H O L A S! I D-D-D-ON'T LI-KE-KE THIS-S-S COM-M-M-M-ERCIAL!!"

Nicky-boy doesn't seem to hear. By now everything is a blur—the trees, the road, even the handwriting on this Last Will and Testament I'm quickly throwing together! In fact, the only thing racing past my eyes faster than the trees and the highway is my life.

Any second now I'll be flying off this cliff. Any second now I'll be heading for that great sketch pad in the sky. Suddenly, like music to my ears, I hear Nick's mom. "Nicholas, come on down for dinner."

Then comes an even better tune: "OK, Mom."

Suddenly everything froze. Nick was done sketching. I looked up to see his grinning face.

"Don't go anywhere, Mop-Top," he chirped as he tossed his art pencil over to the table. "I'll be back after dinner."

"Take all the time you need," I managed to croak. "Maybe afterward Sarah would like some help with the dishes. Oh, and maybe you could help pack Jamie's lunch for tomorrow. Come to think of it, the kitchen could stand a little remodeling, too!"

But he was gone.

And, as soon as I can jimmy this truck door open, I'll be gone, too. Ah, there we go.

Now if I can just find out where he threw that sketch of the pool with the ladies, soda, and pork rinds. . .

SEVEN
"'Cause It's One, Two, Three Strikes . . . "

The last few days before the game were just like the others . . . only worse.

Nick and Louis continued to fall all over themselves as they waited on Thurman hand and foot. I mean, they were doing everything but bowing and calling him "Master." Thurman's slightest wish had become their command. No. Better make that Thurman's slightest whim of a wish had become their command.

And Dad, poor Dad, wasn't doing much better. It seems all he did was think and plan and develop strategies for the upcoming game. When he wasn't thinking and planning he was gloating—over the final destruction of Harvey the Snorter. Yes sir, it was going to be sweet.

On the day before the big game Nicholas brought Thurman over for a little snack. Sarah was sitting at the table going through the mail when the kitchen door flew open and in swaggered Nicholas and his incredible bulky buddy.

Obediently Nick pulled out a chair so the big guy could have a seat. Which put Thurman right in front of Sarah. She looked up and smiled. So this was the super-jock everybody was so ga-ga over. She continued to smile, waiting for some sort of introduction.

Not a word was said.

Sarah waited some more.

Still nothing.

Now the corners around her smile were starting to droop. Somebody better say something. She couldn't keep this smile on forever. But it was becoming more and more obvious that no one was going to say anything. Finally, in an effort to show some sort of friendliness, she cleared her throat and offered a "Hi."

Thurman looked up, surprised. Apparently he hadn't even noticed she was in the room, even though they were only three feet from each other.

"Oh, hi, ahhh . . . ," He was fumbling for a name, any name.

"Sarah," she offered.

"Right," Thurman nodded, acting like he knew it all along.

By now Nick had crossed to the fridge and was peering inside. "Looks like we got chicken salad, apples, meatloaf, banana bread—"

"That'd be fine," Thurman agreed.

Once again Sarah looked up.

"All of it?" Nick asked.

"Sure," Thurman shrugged.

Sarah tried to return to her mail. It was a pretty good batch. One letter even said she was a grand prize winner. All she had to do was come down and claim that prize . . . and of course listen to a 90-minute sales presentation on mobile home vacation campsites on beautiful Lake Hackneehoho. Suddenly Sarah began to suspect junk mail wasn't all it was cracked up to be. So she put all that aside to watch Thurman.

Nick returned to the table, balancing three plates and two bowls. "Here you go," he said as he quickly spread everything before the human eating machine.

Thurman dug in—sometimes chewing, sometimes swallowing . . . but most of the time just inhaling.

Sarah looked on, horrified. Well, horrified *and* fascinated.

Thurman, with his mouth stuffed fuller than humanly possible, began motioning for something to drink.

"Right," Nick said, jumping back to his feet. He raced to the fridge to take another inventory. "We've got cola, chocolate milk, O. J. . . ."

"OK," Thurman mumbled through the chicken salad, apples, and meatloaf.

"All of the above?" Sarah asked dryly. Up until now she had been able to keep quiet. But expecting an older sister to keep her mouth shut through all of this would be as likely as expecting her to fold your socks on wash day.

Thurman grinned. A thick layer of banana bread coated his front teeth. He didn't want Sarah to think he was a pig about the drinks so he compromised. "Cola'd be fine," he called as he caught a piece of chicken trying to escape from the left corner of his mouth.

Immediately Nicholas was at his side, pouring a nice tall glass of cola.

"Where's the ice?" Thurman asked.

"Oh. Right. Ice," Nick answered as he spun around and raced for the freezer compartment of the fridge.

Sarah watched with amazement as Nick threw open the door, fumbled for the ice tray, and fought to pull the handle on it. It was frozen stuck. "Maybe Thurman can help you with that," she offered sarcastically.

Nick was too busy to hear the sarcasm. "No

way!" he insisted as he wrestled with the tray, using every bit of strength he had. "Thurman could strain his arm, or cut his hand, or—OUCH!" Nick stuffed his pinched finger into his mouth and sucked hard to fight off the pain. But pain was no obstacle. Not when it came to pleasing the great Thurman Miller. "We can't have Thurman injured the day before the big game," he insisted.

"Heaven forbid," Sarah muttered under her breath. But before she could say anything more she was interrupted by a huge slurp of cola followed by a gigantic burp.

"Well, thanks, Nick" the human garbage disposal said as he scooted his chair back and slowly rose to his feet. "Gotta go. Hey, did ya get all the dirt out of my cleats?"

Nicholas beamed proudly. "You could eat off those cleats."

"But don't try," Sarah threw in, "you might chip a tooth."

"Yeah, uh, right," Thurman answered, not getting the joke. He turned and started out the door. "See ya tomorrow, Nick."

Nick gave him his best grin.

"And uh, we'll see ya later, uh . . . Karen."

But before Sarah could correct him, the door slammed and he was gone.

It took Sarah a moment to find her voice. "That was unbelievable!" she finally exclaimed.

By now Nicholas had scooped up Thurman's dishes and was dumping them into the sink. "Yeah," he agreed, "he sure can eat."

"I'll say," she marveled. "He practically—" Then

she caught herself. "No . . . I'm not talking about the way he ate . . . I'm talking about the way you fell all over yourself for him! It just doesn't seem right."

"Look," Nicholas argued. "Thurman's like a . . . you know, like a star!"

Sarah could only stare. She had seen Nick get carried away before, but never quite like this.

"Yeah, a star," Nick repeated as he began rinsing the dishes. "You should be proud he even stopped by for a bite."

"A bite?! Godzilla would have done less damage."

Nick could only sigh. How could a big sister that's supposed to be so smart be so dumb?

"Nick." Now she was trying to reason. "Isn't it possible that you're so caught up with Thurman as a baseball player that you can't see what he's like as a person?"

Again Nicholas let out a sigh. It wasn't a great defense but it was about the only one he had.

Sarah did her best to make him see the light. "Don't get me wrong," she tried to explain. "I mean, it's OK to admire someone. . . . But you . . . Nick, you worship the guy. You treat him like he's some kind of idol. And the guy's not even nice!"

"What's being nice got to do with it?"

"Nick. . ."

Nicholas had had just about enough. Sarah was obviously in one of her preaching moods and there would be no reasoning with her. So he turned off the water and headed for the stairs.

"Nick, answer me. . . . Nicholas!"

Finally he turned back to her. She wanted an

answer? All right, he'd give her an answer. "You're just jealous," he shot back. "You're jealous because we're about to become Regional Champs! And you, all you have going for you right now is . . . " He looked around until his eyes landed on the letters in front of her, "Mail!"

Sarah wasn't fazed. In fact, there was something about her that was really sincere. This was more important than their usual brother and sister spats. And she was going to get through to him, no matter how much he tried to hurt her.

"I'm not jealous, Nick." She swallowed hard, then she laid out all the cards. "I'm not jealous . . . but maybe God is."

Nick threw her a look. But she continued.

"*God's* supposed to be the center of our attention," she explained quietly, "He's the one we're supposed to trust . . . remember?"

"Yeah, right, sure," Nicholas countered, not wanting to hear any more. Sarah was starting to make sense, and that was the last thing he wanted or needed. "Just you wait!" he said. "After tomorrow you'll be telling all your friends that Thurman Miller actually spoke to you . . . *Karen!*"

Before Sarah could respond, Nick turned and stormed up the stairs. She watched after him for a long moment. There must be some way she could get through to him—some way she could show him the problem.

Then again, maybe she couldn't. Maybe it would take Someone bigger and better and more loving. Maybe it would take that very Person who wanted to be the center of all of Nick's trust. . . .

EIGHT
"You're Out!"

At last the day of the big game arrived. We're not just talking big game, mind you, we're talking BIG GAME. The Eastfield Braves against the Dodgers. Since Dad ran the local paper, he made sure every radio and TV station in the state knew what was happening. Nothing would please him more than for the whole world to see Harvey the Snorter go down in flames.

Nicholas also had gone to a few extremes, like having Mom wash his uniform three times just in case there were any hidden grass stains he hadn't seen. Then there was the matter of his shoes. He tried and tried to clean up all the scuffs, but nothing seemed to work . . . that is until Louis loaned him his can of white spray paint. Now they were all set. Now nobody would be able to stop them. . . .

"Come on, you're doggin' it!" Dad shouted at his team during the warm-ups in the field. "Do you want to win?"

"Yes!" they shouted.

"Do you want to win?"

"Yes!"

"DO YOU WANT TO WIN?"

"YES!!"

Up in the bleachers Mom, Grandma, Jamie, and Sarah exchanged uneasy glances. They wanted to win, too. But somehow the man shouting at those kids down there was not the same gentle man they loved and respected. Somehow something had happened. In fact, at that moment he seemed a lot like . . . Harvey the Snorter.

"Let's bash 'em!" Harvey was shouting.

"Yes sir!"

"Let's stomp 'em!"

"Yes sir!"

"LET'S TROMP 'EM!"

"YES SIR!"

"Let's play ball!" the umpire shouted.

Dad's team, the Braves, took the field first. A cheer rose up from the crowd as Thurman stalked toward the pitcher's mound and took his stance. Everyone knew what was about to happen . . . especially the frightened batter who was first up for the Dodgers.

Thurman glanced at his watch, stifled a yawn, and started his windup. Exactly two minutes and 24 seconds later, Thurman was heading back to the dugout. He had struck out three batters with three sizzling fast balls apiece! "Can't do any better than that," he shrugged.

But the Dodger pitcher was almost as good as Thurman. And by the third inning the score was still:

Braves—0

Dodgers—0

Then, almost by accident, a Dodger connected with one of Thurman's curves. Unfortunately little Roger Goreman, the wanna-be film director, was playing shortstop. Even more unfortunately, the ball headed directly for him. Now little Roger had two choices, either play it safe and dodge the on-coming ball, or try to catch it. Not being one to take too many chances, ol' Roger decided to leap out of the way.

But the ball still managed to hit him, and by the time he found it and picked it up, the batter was nearly to first.

"Throw it! Throw it!" the first baseman yelled.

Roger threw it. Unfortunately he missed his mark by about fifteen feet and everyone watched as the ball sailed high into the grandstands.

Meanwhile, the runner, who could have come into second standing up, thought it would be great to show off with a little slide . . . a slide that knocked second baseman Louis off his feet and high into the air.

Immediately Dad was out on the field shouting about the unnecessary roughness, and immedi-ately one of the umpires was in his face shouting at him to cool it.

Mom glanced away, embarrassed.

Thurman was so upset because the kid got a double off him that he walked the next three run-ners and hit the fourth. Finally, after a little talk on the pitcher's mound, Dad was able to settle him down to finish the inning. But the damage was already done. The score at the end of the third inning was:

Braves—0
Dodgers—2

By the fifth inning, Nick had struck out once and grounded out once. Now he was up to bat again. Things would be different this time. Dad had given him a big pep talk just before he left the dugout, and now the kid was ready to do some major damage. He stepped into the batting box, took a few manly practice swings, and did his best to look mean and ferocious at the pitcher.

Three swings and three strikes later, Nick was heading back to the dugout, having done no damage and definitely not feeling all that mean or ferocious.

Dad was not pleased with Nick and showed it.

Mom was not pleased with Dad and tried not to show it.

Harvey was pleased with everyone and snorted in glee.

Things got even more interesting for the next three innings. Dad's team pressed in hard and actually managed to score five runs! Two of them were courtesy of Thurman Miller's mighty biceps; the other three came from kids lucky enough to be on base when those biceps belted out their homers. It was incredible . . . terrific . . . fantastic!

The only problem was Harvey's team had also scored five more runs. It was awful . . . unbelievable . . . dreadful!

The score by the end of the eighth inning was:

Braves—5
Dodgers—7

Finally the ninth inning rolled around. Dad's team was still behind by two runs, but any second now they were expecting—

Hold it, wait a minute, Bub. What say we let a real storyteller tell this tallish tale, shall we? After all, I was there. I saw it, I heard it, I lived it. Yes sir, you guessed it—it is I, the world-famous poet, Henry Wadsworth McGeefellow. Being such a famous former of phrases and a renown wrangler of rhymes, what better way for me to tell this epic story than with a praiseworthy poem?

So, sit back and get ready for some real culture.

Ahem . . . Ladies and Gentlemen, Guys and Guyettes, it is with dynamically dramatic talent (and sincerely apologetic apologies to the real poet, Earnest Lawrence Thayer), that I recite "Casey—", er, make that "Thurman at the Bat."

> "It looked extremely rocky
>   for the Eastfield nine that day;
> The score stood 5 to 7
>   with an inning left to play.
> So, when Eddie died at second,
>   and Peter did the same,
> A pallor weathered the features
>   of the patrons of the game.
>
> "A straggling few got up to go, *(those rotten, no-good traitors)*
>   leaving there the rest,
> With that hope that springs eternal
>   within the human breast.

For they thought: 'If only Thurman
    could get a crack at that,'
They'd put money even now,
    with Thurman at the bat."

Pretty good so far, huh? Hang on, it gets better . . .

"Then Nick let drive a single,
    to the wonderment of all.
And the understated Louis
    tore the cover off the ball.
And when the dust had lifted,
    and they saw what had occurred,
There was Louis safe at second,
    And Nick a-huggin' third."

Atta baby, Nick! All right, Louis! Nice work guys!

"Then from the gladdened multitude
    went up a joyous yell—
It rumbled in the mountaintops,
    it rattled in the dell;
It struck upon the hillside
    and rebounded on the flat;
For Thurman, mighty Thurman,
    was advancing to the bat."

All right, Thurmmy!

"There was ease in Thurman's manner
    as he stepped into his place,
There was pride in Thurman's bearing
    and a smile upon his face;

And when responding to the cheers
    he lightly tipped his hat,
No stranger in the crowd
    could doubt it's Thurman at the bat.

"Ten thousand eyes were on him . . ."

OK, so there were only three or four hundred.
Sheesh! Haven't you ever heard of poetic license?

"Ten thousand eyes were on him . . .
    as he rubbed his hands with dirt,
Five thousand tongues applauded
    when he wiped them on his shirt;
Then when the writhing pitcher
    ground the ball into his hip,
Defiance glanced in Thurman's eye,
    a sneer curled Thurman's lip.

"And now the leather-covered sphere
    came hurtling through the air,
And Thurman stood a-watching it
    in haughty grandeur there.
Close by the sturdy batsman
    the ball unheeded sped; *(the puppy was*
    flying!)
'That ain't my style,' said Thurman.
    'Strike one,' the umpire said.

"From the benches full of people,
    there went up a muffled roar,
Like the beating of the storm waves
    on the stern and distant shore.

'Kill him! Kill the umpire!'
  shouted someone on the stand;
And it's likely they'd have killed him
  had not Thurman raised his hand.

"With a smile of noble charity
  great Thurman's visage shone;
  (Translation: The guy was cool.)
He stilled the rising tumult,
  he made the game go on;
He signaled to the pitcher,
  and once more the spheroid flew;
But Thurman still ignored it,
  and the umpire said, 'Strike two.'

"'Fraud!' cried the maddened thousands,
  and the echo answered 'Fraud!'
But one scornful look from Thurman
  and the audience was awed;
They saw his face grow stern and cold,
  they saw his muscles strain,
And they knew that Thurman wouldn't let
  the ball go by again.

"The sneer is gone from Thurman's lips,
  his teeth are clenched in hate,
He pounds with cruel vengeance
  his bat upon the plate;
And now the pitcher holds the ball,
  and now he lets it go,
And now the air is shattered
  by the force of Thurman's blow . . ."

And blow it did. I tell you, when that guy finished swinging it was like a mini-hurricane. Hats blew away, and toupees blew off. It was incredible! But not incredible enough. Let's see, where was I? Oh, yeah . . .

> "Oh, somewhere in this favored land
>   the sun is shining bright,
> The band is playing somewhere
>   and somewhere hearts are light;
> And men like Harvey snort with glee,
>   and somewhere children shout;
> But there is no joy for Nick . . . or
>   Dad . . . or Eastfield:
>   The Mighty Thurman has struck out."

Yep, you guessed her, Chester. Ol' Thurman baby went down swinging. No one could believe it, not Dad, not Nick, not Louis, and most of all not Thurmmy.

Yes-siree-bob, Nick's team lost—and in a big way. It was a dark day for everyone. Well, almost everyone. Harvey the Snorter seemed to be having a pretty good time. And, lucky for me, I discovered the concession stand had a two-for-one close-out sale. So I wasn't suffering as much as you'd expect.

By the way, anyone know what I can do with 247 hot dogs and 1.3 tons of stale popcorn?

NINE
"At the Old Ball Game"

Dad wasn't sure how long it had been since the game had ended. It could have been minutes, it could have been hours. He just didn't know.

What he did know was that the overflowing crowd had now been reduced to just two concession people sweeping up; that all the cheering and clapping had been reduced to quiet rustlings of empty popcorn bags and used Pepsi cups; and what had once been the Mighty Coach of the Mighty Braves was now just a lonely man sitting near the pitcher's mound staring at home plate. A man who felt humbled, defeated, and, yes, even a little silly.

Without a word Nick slowly approached and sat beside his father.

"How we doing?" Dad asked, still staring straight ahead.

Nick looked over his shoulder to the scoreboard where their agonizing defeat remained etched in

vivid black-and-white numbers. "Still losing," he said with a sigh.

Dad glanced at his son. There was no missing the catch in the boy's voice or the red in his eyes from crying. In an instant Dad had his arm out and was pulling Nicholas toward him.

Nick let him. To be honest, a good hug right now wasn't such a bad idea. After a moment, Dad spoke. "You know . . . I've been sitting here thinking about how bad I wanted this game. You know, beat Harvey the Snorter, manage a championship team . . . maybe conquer the world."

Nicholas tried to smile, but without much luck.

"I tell you," Dad said with a sigh as he looked back to home plate, "it sure seemed like we had all the ingredients."

"Especially Thurman Miller," Nick nodded.

After another pause Dad continued. "Well, son, I think we both found out that when you dream without the Lord . . . you'd better dream again."

Nick was already nodding. He remembered all too clearly his argument with Sarah after he'd waited on Thurman hand and foot. "Someone tried to tell me that a couple days back," he answered, "but I wouldn't—"

"You guys OK?"

The fellows looked up to see Sarah approaching. Right beside her was Mom.

"We got a little worried," Mom added, "I mean, when you didn't show at home."

Dad and Nick each gave a little shrug, almost in unison.

"Aw . . . ," Mom said. She offered her hand to

help Dad stand. He took it and once he was on his feet she gave him a reassuring hug. "How you doing, Coach?"

"Oh, a little better," Dad answered.

"You OK?" It was Sarah and she was speaking to Nick. In fact, she was even putting her arm around him.

"Yeah," he said as he looked down a little embarrassed. In their fight he had put her down left and right. Now it was all too clear that she had just been trying to help. He knew that—now. And he knew that if he had listened to her, things might have been different. Boy, did he know it. At last he looked up at her. "Listen, I'm sorry about the other day. . . . I, uh—"

"No problem," she smiled.

For the first time that afternoon, Nick was also able to smile. For an older sister, Sarah wasn't bad. Not bad at all.

By now Mom had her arm around Dad and was starting to direct him back to the car. "Time to re-enter the human race, sweetheart. You too, Nick."

By now both guys were feeling better. Mom was right. They had wallowed long enough in their pity party. Now it was time to get going—to get back into the game . . . of life.

They both knew they'd made some mistakes. Some Triple-A, megaton mistakes. Fortunately they knew the Lord—and their family—would forgive them. So it was time to get up, learn from those mistakes, and carry on.

They also knew there'd be other mistakes—some even bigger than their Thurman disaster. But that was OK, because with the Lord as their "coach," those mistakes would never become major defeats. They'd just be "golden opportunities" for learning and growing.

Of course, none of that really helped make things hurt less. At least, not yet. But it did help everything make more sense.

Well, guys and gals, thus endeth another fun-filled, action-packed, nearly-all-expenses-paid adventure into the life and times of me and my buddy. I tell you, Nick could sure save himself a lot of trouble by asking me for advice. But I guess some things you gotta learn on your own.

Anyways, to all you jocks and jockettes out there, take care. We'll see you soon for our next exciting trip into the eerie and uncharted life of Nicky "Boy Wonder" Martin. Oh, and be sure to bring your appetites. No promises, but there still just might be a couple of these 247 hot dogs left from the game.

CHOMP-CHOMP, BURP, *Ahhhh. . . .*

Make that 246. Better hurry, they're going fast. . . .